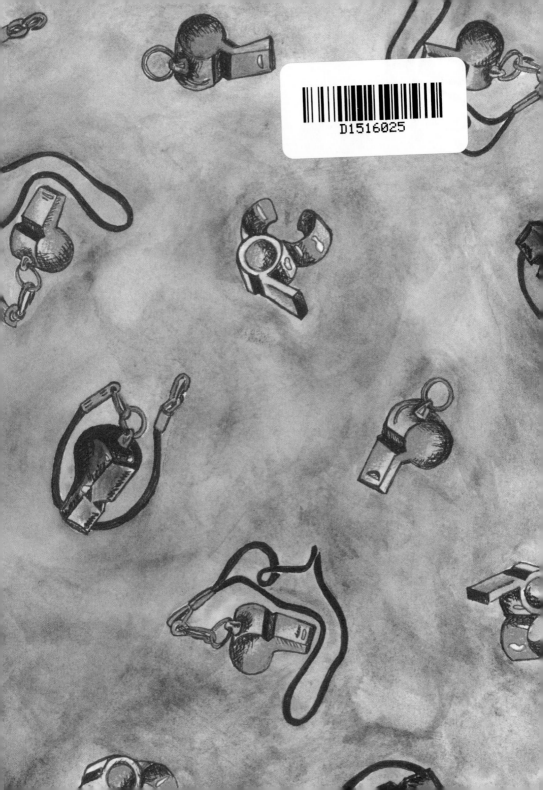

Praise for *The Official Adventures Series* and *Drop the Puck, Hooray for Hockey Day!*

"The Official Adventures book series is special to our family. The books teach real life lessons and the joys of hockey, family, and teammates. Hockey Day is a special holiday to all of us in Minnesota. We love these books!"

Matt and Bridget Cullen, three-time Stanley Cup Champion

"These chapter books are terrific! The love of hockey and friends rings true throughout them. We love the idea of Hockey Day as a Minnesota holiday!"

Jordan and Jamie Leopold, former NHL player and parents of Paisley and Team Leopold

"Playing hockey with the Washington Ice Dogs is amazing, awesome, cool...all the good words! And it's also awesome that my friends, Ann and Rick Nash, are in the book too!"

Aiden Plummer "Chop Chop," Washington Ice Dogs

"It's super cool playing hockey with my friends. I love skating, meeting new friends, and cheering for the Caps! A book about hockey, the Ice Dogs, and my dream of being the Capitals announcer is a hat trick of awesomeness!"

Ann Schaab, Washington Ice Dogs

"Like all Minnesotans, we vote yes for Hockey Day and treasure the friendships hockey gives to all players! Keep reading!"

Phil and Sen. Karin Housley, Buffalo Sabers

ISBN 13: 978-1-63489-141-7
LCCN: 2018947821
Printed in the United States of America
First Printing: 2018

22 21 20 19 18   5 4 3 2 1

Book design and typesetting by Tiffany Daniels.

Wise Ink Creative Publishing
837 Glenwood Avenue
Minneapolis, MN 55405
wiseinkpub.com

To order, visit www.itascabooks.com or call 1-800-901-3480.
Reseller discounts available.

Drop the Puck
Hooray for Hockey Day!

THE OFFICIAL ADVENTURES

Written by Jayne J. Jones Beehler
Illustrated by Katrina G. Dohm

For friendships, on and off the ice.

A Note from Jayne and Katrina

The Official Adventures Series, showcasing brothers Blaine and Cullen, continues with this fourth tale. Blaine and Ann were born with Down syndrome and have special needs. Down syndrome is a genetic disorder that can cause physical growth delays, characteristic facial features, and mild to moderate intellectual disability. Blaine and Ann's speech at times can be stuttering, slurring, and repetitive.

Get ready! It's time to cheer loud and proud—*Drop the Puck, Hooray for Hockey Day!*

The Official Adventures Book Series:

And the story goes...
for the love of the game.

CHAPTER 1

Hockey Day Eve

*I*t was a bitterly cold Hockey Day Eve in Hockeytown, USA. Stanley Cup, a bulldog with a rather unusual name, sniffed the snow boots in Luke's mudroom, licking moisture from the edges.

"Look! It's Jeremy Roenick's Hawks rookie card!" exclaimed Cullen, who'd transformed into a kid in a candy store. He and Luke were sorting their mile-high

collections of pro hockey player cards—
when Luke wasn't looking, Cullen would
sneak a trade. Their other teammates were
scattered around the floor and engulfed
by paper and markers, creating signs for
their Hockey Day concession stand.

"I think Hockey Day should be a
national holiday!" Avery declared,

adding yet another layer of red to her sign's lettering.

"Isn't it already? In Minnesota, at least?" Paisley asked, glancing up from her scribbling.

"No, not an actual holiday. But at our house, we hang our game day socks up with care, like stockings on the mantel!" Cullen said, laughing, and reached toward Luke's pile of cards.

Luke slapped Cullen's hand away. "We should petition Capitol Hill for an official Hockey Day! Like Ms. Marvin taught us about," he said.

"Us kids? Doing that?" asked Paisley, with a marker hanging from her fingers.

"We burn popcorn in the concession stand. You think we can get Hockey Day as a holiday?" Cullen said doubtfully.

"I love holidays! With presents! Lots of presents!" snickered Ann.

"Yeessss, lottss of presents. Pllllusss nooooo school on Hockey Day!" Blaine cheered.

Ann leapt up and triumphantly began to march in place. "I vote YES for Hockey Day!"

"We better not quit our day jobs just yet, Senators!" Avery cautioned, gesturing at the signage that covered the floor.

"Sen-a-tors? We are the Bears!" Ann corrected. "Not the Senators."

"But us going to Capitol Hill? The Bears skating outside the Capitol would be cool!" Paisley said.

"Coooooollll," echoed Blaine.

Eager to change the subject, Cullen seized the sign Blaine was working on. "What does that say?"

4

"'Buy sushi for ASHA!'" Ann proudly read out loud.

"Sushi? Since when does a hockey rink concession stand have sushi?" asked Luke.

"That's a big shift from the concessions I thought we were going to offer. Where's the popcorn, mini donuts, and hot dogs?" Paisley asked, scooting closer to help with the sign-making.

"I-I-I-I loovvee mini donuts, I'mmmm having them for Hockkkkey Dayyyy breakfassstt, llunnchh and dinnnnnerrr!" Blaine exclaimed. The entire group of friends giggled.

"It's a holiday now! Only the best! We serve sushi!" said Ann.

"Ugh, sushi rolls mixed with smelly hockey bags," Avery groaned. "I might throw up." Paisley pretended to gag.

"We better stick to the original list," said Luke.

"You mean high-sticking?" Ann pretended to blow a referee's whistle. Blaine joined the fun by motioning the high-sticking penalty sign.

"Ref Rylee would be impressed," Cullen said, "but we want to sell food! Sushi doesn't make the cut."

"I wonder if Ref Rylee and Ref

Rosee are officiating our outdoor game tomorrow?" Paisley said. "They better wear earmuffs under their helmets!"

"My dad said the temperature is only supposed to be 5 below zero!" said Luke.

"That's nothing. Cold air all feels the same. What matters is we'll be on an Olympic size-sheet of outdoor ice. Best day ever!" said Cullen.

Avery laughed. "I might need three pairs of long johns and some skate heaters."

"Someone better warn Jagger Stephen! He'll need to grow a beard overnight, like his dad!" Cullen giggled.

"His dad's beard is awesome! Will it freeze?" Ann asked. The friends all giggled at the image of a beard frozen over and spikey with icicles, then returned to their work.

CHAPTER 2

Hockeytown, USA or Bust

Hockey Day was a combined make-believe holiday and hockey camp reunion that took place in the skating haven of Hockeytown, USA. From sunrise to sundown, Hockey Day brought unlimited hours of play, thrills, and joys for the teams battling for the cherished Hockey Day Trophy. Old traditions were observed and new traditions were born. And as Hockey Day's host town, Hockeytown, USA had added a special hockey festival with pro players as volunteer coaches.

As the festivities drew closer, players and refs alike were ready to Drop the Puck.

The hotel was overflowing with all manner of ice-related odds and ends. "You couldn't squeeze another hockey bag in this place," Ref Rosee joked with the front desk clerk, smiling. "This town sure lives up to its name!" She and Ref Rylee carefully wove their way through scattered hockey sticks, bags, and crowds of young players finding their hotel rooms.

Jagger Stephen and McLaren, along with their teammates, poured out of their team vans. McLaren instantly buried his face in his gloves. Jagger Stephen gasped and started choking on the bitterly cold air. "Are we in Minnesota or Antarctica?" he said with a chuckle.

"Now this is what I call cold!" McLaren's dad howled. Jagger Stephen laughed as he read his first text from Cullen: "'Don't stick your tongue to a metal pole or the nets! See you at the rink!'"

Before they'd made it into the hotel, the team all stopped in their tracks. A sign had caught their attention: *No hockey in the hotel halls after 11 pm*. "Rockin' Rangers! We can play floor hockey at this hotel!" Jagger Stephen cheered.

"Team, we have *arrived* in Hockeytown, USA!" McLaren shouted as the players took a picture of the sign.

"The town with more goal lights than stoplights!" added Jagger Stephen.

Welcome to Hockeytown USA and Hockey Day Minnesota 2018
No Hockey in the hotel halls after 11 pm

The team huddled around their coach. Room assignments were announced and room keys handed out. The coach explained hotel etiquette and expectations. "There's no running, shouting, roughhousing, or horseplay. You must wear your team warm-up for breakfast, which is at 6 a.m. sharp."

"6 a.m.?" McLaren asked, incredulous. The team moaned.

"We're here for Hockey Day, not playing cribbage in the lobby!" the coach responded, adding, "And lights out by 10 p.m." When more moans echoed: "We can pack up our hockey bags and head back home right now."

As the teams broke up, McLaren turned to his friend. "What time does the pool close?" he asked. "Think we still have a shot?"

"Grab your trunks," ordered Jagger Stephen. "Be in the pool in five minutes."

The swimming pool was packed. "Who's game for a belly flop contest?" McLaren asked, surveying the dozens of kids bobbing in the water.

Hands rose across the pool. "Meeeeeee!" a young boy with a bright smile exclaimed.

The boy instantly climbed out of the pool. McLaren and Jagger Stephen couldn't help but stare at him.

"Rock, paper, scissors to see who goes first?" he invited. "I might only have one leg, but it's a strong one!" He tensed the muscles in his single lower limb for emphasis; the other ended in a stump

just above where the knee should have been.

"I'm Aiden," he added by way of introduction. "Some people call me Chop Chop, because I'm fast and a foodie!"

"I-I-I'm McLaren," McLaren bashfully responded.

"What team?" Aiden inquired.

"Team?"

"Your hockey team? You know, Hockey Day?" The other boy grinned teasingly. "I *am* in the right town? More goal lights than stoplights? This *is* Hockeytown, USA?"

"He plays for the Junior Rangers with us," Jagger Stephen jumped in.

"Cool! I play for the Washington Ice Dogs," Aiden answered. Then, without warning, he squatted and dove into the pool—a picture-perfect belly flop.

McLaren and Jagger Stephen looked at each other. "He skates?" Jagger Stephen quietly asked.

"Probably better than you," McLaren replied.

"Magnificent, Chop Chop!" Jagger Stephen yelled at Aiden with a thumbs-up.

"Of course I skate!" the other boy shouted back. "Who doesn't skate in Hockeytown, USA?" He snickered.

"Well, then, we'll see you at the rink!" Jagger Stephen shouted.

"Yes, see you at the rink!" Aiden hooted back.

CHAPTER

3

Hockey Day Perfection

With the sunrise glowing over the two outdoor rinks and Warroad Gardens lighting up the center of the city like a beacon, Hockeytown, USA had never looked better. Television crews busily set up satellites to capture all the games.

"Do you smell that?" Ref Rylee asked Ref Rosee, sniffing the air as they strode

across one of the sheets of ice, basking in the morning glow.

"Smell it? We live it!" said Ref Rosee, throwing her arms wide to encompass the whole arena.

"Every rink has its own smell. I could walk in and pick out the Gardens without even opening my eyes!" Ref Rylee inhaled deeply.

"I think maybe you've been refereeing too much hockey lately," Ref Rosee said, chuckling.

"No, it's true. I could win big on a game show—*Smell That Rink!*" Another deep breath.

"Look!" said Ref Rosee, pointing forward. "Here's the Officials' Locker Room!"

"Luke, did you take Stanley Cup out?" his dad asked.

"He won't go outside!" Luke yelled back, stuffing equipment into his hockey bag.

"What? Why?"

"It's too cold for him!"

"We have to be at the rink in twenty minutes! Get that bulldog outside!"

Luke sighed and turned to the bulldog, who was looking with trepidation at the falling snow outside. "Listen buddy, you need to go outside," Luke reasoned with his pet. "When we leave for Hockey Day, I'll leave the TV on. You can watch us and hockey all day!"

Stanley Cup wagged his stubby tail, tilted his head, and barked. "Boy, oh boy! We gave you the right name from the start, Stanley Cup!" Luke said, stroking him.

"Cullen! Cullen! It'sssss Hockkeey Dayy!"
Blaine cheered.

"I'm so fired up!" Cullen replied,
stuffing the last of his gear into his bag.

"Meeee toooo!"

"Two days of just hockey. You're going to be busy!" He swept the bag up onto his shoulder. "Between being our team manager, playing for the Minnesota Bears, and helping in the concession stand, you should pack a sleeping bag and just stay overnight at the rink!"

"Yeessssss! I-I-I-I shoulddddddd!" Blaine high-fived his brother.

"No overnights at the rink!" their mom said, laughing.

"I-I-I-I-I could sleeeppp and showerrr in the locker room. Coooolll." Blaine said, attempting to persuade her.

Their mom shook her head, smiling. "Boys, in the car in five minutes—*without* sleeping bags!"

"A little higher on the right side," Cullen instructed Avery, who arched her tiptoes even further up as she struggled with the sign and a roll of tape.

"Nice of you to finally show up," Paisley said, tapping her watch. She shifted the concession-stand signs she was helping Avery tape to the rink walls, careful not to drop them on the already-mud-stained floor.

Luke peeked into the roasters of nacho meat. "Wow! This concession stand sure is fancy." He leaned in closer. "I'm sure the food will be tasty—"

"No freebies!" Avery barked, pushing Luke's nose away.

"I hope we sell out of e-v-e-r-y-t-h-i-n-g! And raise a lot of loot for the special hockey and the Bears!" Paisley cheered.

"I love volunteering," Avery said,

slapping a final piece of tape onto the corner of her sign. "And working the concession stand rocks!"

"Meeee too!! Minniiii donuts for evvverryyoone!" exclaimed Blaine.

"Don't forget, your first job is scoring back-to-back hat tricks on the ice, Avery!" said Cullen.

"Sheeeeee willlll!" Blaine high-fived Avery.

Ann and her mom arrived to work the first shift. "Where's the sushi?" Ann asked, sliding behind the counter.

"Doooon't worry! Weeee gooottt miinnnii donnuttts!" Blaine informed her.

"Holy hockey breezers!" Jagger Stephen crowed.

"Now this is what I call a hockey

palace!" McLaren said, staring at the outdoor rinks as the two boys and their teammates filed into the specially designed Hockey Day Campus.

"Look at those snow sculptures!" Jagger Stephen said, pointing into the distance.

"That's the Stanley Cup! And that's a mini replica of the Mount State of Hockey!" McLaren shouted.

"Far out! This is so cool," Jagger Stephen exclaimed, taking pictures like a tourist. The town really did live and breathe hockey.

Everyone had arrived for Hockey Day!

Hockey Day Battles

Hockey Day's first match pitted friends against friends, with Hockeytown, USA playing the Junior Rangers.

"Team, we have a double header. Our game is live on State of Hockey television!" Cullen pumped up his teammates.

"This is no time for crashing into the boards, tripping on our own blue line, or missing the net," Luke added.

"This is our rink. Our house. We play big for Hockeytown, USA all day!" Avery cheered. The teammates came together in a huddle and raised their fists.

"We play every shift. *Champions* play every shift," said Cullen.

"We stay out of the penalty box," said Paisley.

"We work hard. Skate hard. Shoot hard," said Luke.

"We play as a team—everyone matters. Every *play* matters," Avery said.

"Onnnn threeee!" Blaine concluded.

"Hockeytown, USA!" the entire team hollered, charging out of the locker room.

"This is unbelievable," Jagger Stephen said to McLaren as the Junior Rangers lined up.

Fans and reporters crowded around the outdoor ice rink.

"I won't need any skate warmers. The energy here is like an outdoor furnace built inside my skates. This place is on fire!" McLaren roared.

Ref Rylee opened the rink door. He gave the official approval for the teams to enter the ice.

"I wish I had a helmet cam!" Jagger Stephen shouted.

"To capture all my goals against you?" Cullen asked from the center line.

"Good one!" Jagger Stephen said, rolling his eyes.

After the warm-ups ended, Ref Rylee and Ref Rosee gathered at center ice. The stadium speakers played the national anthem and the teams were introduced.

"I've never seen hockey hair like that

before," said Jagger Stephen, looking quizzically at the other team's disheveled heads.

"Maybe the town's barber population is equal to its stoplights," McLaren joked.

"Hockeytown, USA is the crown jewel of hockey hair," Cullen stated as he positioned himself for the first faceoff. "We'll see who's laughing once the game is over."

"Sticks down, heads up," Ref Rosee said, dropping the puck.

Ann counted on her fingers. "Five dollars, please!" she said.

"That's correct, Ann! Great job!" her mom exclaimed. The customer gave Ann a twenty-dollar bill.

Ann whispered to her mom, "She gets ten dollars back?"

"Twenty minus five is . . . ?" Ann's mom prompted.

"I know. I know. I can do it," Ann whispered again.

"Take your time," her mom encouraged.

Ann tilted her head to the side for a moment. ". . . fifteen!"

The customer smiled. "I'll make you a deal. Why don't you just give me five dollars back? You can keep the other ten dollars for the Minnesota Bears!"

"Wow! That's awesome! Special hockey is sweet. I like playing. I want to be captain of my team," Ann said joyfully.

"That's terrific! I'm glad you play for the Bears—you'd make a great captain," the customer said with a wink.

"Yes, I would!" Ann said with a big smile.

Her mom nudged her. "What?" Ann whispered, confused. Her mom gave her a clarifying look.

"Oh yeah!" She turned back to the customer. "Thank you! My teammates will be happy! You're nice!"

"You are too!"

"You did an excellent job, Ann!" her mom reassured her as the customer walked away.

Ann sighed. "I don't like math."

"You just added and subtracted in seconds. Playing for the Minnesota Bears is giving you stamina on *and* off the ice!"

"What is sta-min-a?" Ann questioned.

"Stamina! It means your attention span is increasing and getting sharper. You've improved in your math skills and your homework. Plus, you can play longer on the ice without needing a break!"

"That's cool. I still don't like math. I love hockey! When I grow up, I'm going to be the announcer for the Washington Capitals! I know every player and number. That's my kind of math!" Ann declared.

"Those are my kind of goals!" her mom replied.

"I can't believe we're going to a shoot-out in game one!" Ref Rylee exclaimed. "Pee Wee hockey at its best!"

After three regulation periods and

one sudden-death overtime, the game remained tied at 6-6. Scoring the goals for Hockeytown, USA were Avery, Luke, and Cullen, who had two goals each. For the Junior Rangers, both McLaren and Jagger Stephen had hat-tricks. Cullen had managed to stay out of the penalty box, but Paisley had received a ten-minute penalty for slamming her stick against the boards.

"Each team selects three players for the first round of the shoot-out. If there's no winner, we'll proceed to round two!" Ref Rylee explained to the teams' captains.

For the first round of the shoot-out, Hockeytown, USA selected Luke, Cullen, and Avery. For the Junior Rangers, McLaren and Jagger Stephen made the cut along with a defenseman.

"Let'ssss wwwwinnnn and fffinish thissss! Myyyy handssss are ffffrozennnn," Blaine cheered after refilling the team's water bottles.

All six skaters scored in the first round of the shoot-out. "In round two, we play sudden death. First team that scores wins! We will flip a coin to see who shoots first," Ref Rosee told the captains.

"I call heads," Jagger Stephen said.

After a few moments: "Tails it is!" Ref Rosee announced.

Hockeytown, USA selected Avery as their first shooter. As Avery began to skate forward, her left skate got caught in a large rut on the outdoor ice. Avery instantly fell before taking a good shot.

Her wrist shot was short. Her teammates looked sad.

McLaren skated to center ice and took a deep breath. He powered forward, rifled a slap shot, and scored.

Hockeytown, USA had lost their first game.

CHAPTER 5

Grab Those Skates and Go

"The Minnesota Bears and Washington Ice Dogs play next on ice rink #2," announced Luke's dad. "You're up, guys!"

"Every time you get the puck, will you pass to me?" Ann asked Blaine.

"Onnlllyy ifff youuuu takkeee a shoottt!" Blaine quickly answered as his mom helped him lace up his skates.

"Can we fill our water bottles with hot cocoa to stay warm?" Ann suggested to her mom.

"Yesss! And marshhhhhhmellows!" Blaine added.

Ann's mom smiled. "Well, that could make them awfully sticky, but I'll see what I can do."

Blaine leaned toward her and whispered. "I'mmmmmm neerrrvvous."

"We are here to have fun, make new friends, and play hockey," Ann's mom replied, handing Ann her water bottle and helmet. "No need to be nervous!"

"Let's go Bears!" Ann cheered.

Together, the teammates marched onto the ice. After a long, straight glide, Blaine wiped out on the outdoor ice.

"Get up, Blaine! We can't score any goals sitting down!" Ann rallied.

"Oh, yes you can!" Aiden yelled as he whizzed by the duo.

"Whooooaa, loookkkk," Blaine said, pointing. Ann struggled to get her mom's attention—Aiden was skating on ice sledge hockey equipment, racing around the rink faster than any other players. The metal frame underneath him zoomed across the ice, propelled by two sticks that the little boy wielded expertly.

"Cooooolllll," Blaine said, astounded, before struggling to his feet.

Hockeytown, USA teammates joined the Junior Rangers on the bleachers for the special hockey festival. In special hockey games, there are no icings or off-sides. Slap shots are not allowed. A whistle is blown and a face-off occurs as volunteer referees dictate. Play is non-checking and only incidental contact is allowed. Goalies are encouraged to keep the puck in play.

"Oh my gosh! I think Aiden is faster than Cullen," Paisley roared as she spotted Avery a seat.

"Paging Hockeytown, USA Ice Patrol, we have a speed skater on rink #2 and his name's not Cullen!" Avery joked.

"Remarkably rad! Way to go, Chop Chop!" whooped Jagger Stephen.

The special hockey players continued to warm up, Aiden dashing across the ice at faster and faster speeds.

"I'd love to see a skills competition showdown, Chop Chop versus Cullen," McLaren suggested.

"My money's on Chop Chop," Luke said.

"Mine too!" agreed Cullen, laughing.

"Go Ann! Go Blaine!" called Paisley and Avery, applauding.

"Dad! Dad! Up here!" yelled Jagger Stephen, trying to get his dad's attention as he videotaped the Ice Dogs' players gathered on the team bench.

"Now, ladies and gents, my money is on the Minnesota Bears!" Avery high-fived Paisley, then turned to the bench to watch their dads, ready to coach.

"This is hockey at its best," McLaren said. "Even though our dads play pro and we've been to a million games, being here right now, seeing them coach these special hockey teams, is incredible!" He wiped away a tear that had welled up in his eye.

"Hockey is truly a game for everyone," Luke said.

"You got that right!" Paisley banged the boards, encouraging Blaine.

"Missing the shoot-out goal today and then throwing a tantrum in the locker room would seem ridiculous and minimal for this game," Avery observed. "It's the playing that matters."

The teammates and friends watched every minute, cheering for both teams and applauding their remarkable skills, talent, and persistence.

"Dad! Coach! Dad! Coach!" Avery and Paisley yelled together while pointing down the ice. "Blaine, as the cherry picker!"

The coaches jumped onto the team's bench and bellowed to the players, "Go!"

Ann passed the puck, nearly missing Aiden's stick blade. A drop pass to Blaine, it was spot-on—its recipient was perfectly positioned as a cherry picker in front of the Ice Dogs' net.

Goal! The game was tied.

"Listen, Ice Dogs, we got this! I'll even

dye my beard red, white, and blue tonight if you win this one for us," Jagger Stephen's dad said. "That's a promise."

"Don't you worry, Coach! I got our backs—I'll shoot it right through the pipes!" Aiden said with a grin.

And just like that, Chop Chop hustled, skating from the farthest corner of the rink to its opposite, coast to coast. With a *smack* he shot the puck into the net, scoring the game-winning goal.

"Special hockey rocks!" exclaimed Jagger Stephen's dad to McLaren's dad.

"Yes it does! What a snipe! A great win and even better players!" McLaren's dad said.

"Race you to get mini donuts!" Ann challenged Blaine as she unlaced the last of her gear.

"Yummmmmm!" Blaine responded, running out of locker room.

CHAPTER 6

Hockey Day Breakaways

"The concession stand is cleaned and ready for tomorrow's games!" Ann's mom celebrated.

"I loved it! I loved collecting money!" Ann winked.

"Anddddd tassttttyyy work!" Blaine added.

"We sold a lot of hot dogs and mini

donuts! We raised major money for special hockey!" Paisley exclaimed as she helped Avery count the stand's money.

"Hi there!" Jagger Stephen said, walking up to the stand and pulling some crumpled bills from his wallet. "I'll take eight bags of mini donuts, please."

"Eight—*eight* bags?" Ann asked.

"Just like my dad's lucky number. Eight bags of mini donuts brings eight sweet, hot goals tomorrow!" Jagger Stephen said.

"You better start eating more than just eight! Try eighty-eight!" Cullen joked.

"Weeeeee arreee clossssed," Blaine interjected.

"Closed?" Jagger Stephen whined.

"But we'll still take your money—you said eighty-eight bags?" Avery asked, guffawing.

"We were going to bring them back to the hotel—to share with Aiden and the Ice Dogs," McLaren said.

"Cool," said Ann.

"Fuuuuunnn," Blaine stated, rubbing his stomach.

"Even Blaine can't eat eight bags of mini donuts!" Paisley said.

"Yeessss I cannn," Blaine replied.

"We love that idea! Here's a few leftover goodies and treats from today, you can share," Ann's mom offered.

"Groovy!" Jagger Stephen answered. McLaren took the box of treats.

"Sounds like a party to me!" Avery said, dancing.

"Holy cow, you guys," exclaimed Luke from the side. "For real? We made $3,088 today!"

"Woooowwww!" Blaine cheered, spinning around.

"Too cool for hockey school," Cullen said.

After officiating five games, Ref Rylee joined Ref Rosee in the hotel lobby. "A well-spent Hockey Day!" The two high-fived.

"Incredible competition, joyful players, and stellar sportsmanship," Ref Rosee summarized the day.

"That's a hat-trick!" Ref Rylee said, laughed, and dodged a foam puck.

"You can take the hockey players out of the rink, but you can't take the hockey out of the players."

The hotel lobby and pool area quickly

became a makeshift floor hockey rink.
The Ice Dogs befriended the Junior
Rangers. Aiden, Jagger Stephen, and
McLaren played hallway floor hockey
and card games and laughed until just
shy of their coach's curfew.

Just as things were starting to wind
down, Jagger Stephen's dad entered the
lobby. As he stepped out of the shadows
into the light, the players couldn't help
but notice that something was . . .
different about his appearance.

"Radical!" Jagger Stephen exclaimed,
grabbing his cell phone.

Aiden just looked on, gaping.

Ref Rosee couldn't control her
laughter.

"Is that permanent?" asked McLaren.

"Taking Hockey Day to the extreme,
eh?" asked Ref Rylee.

"Red, white, and blue! Just like my team ordered!" Jagger Stephen's dad exclaimed, stroking his colorful beard. The mop of hair had gone from dull brown to a vivid three-color rainbow.

"Don't move, Dad! This will go viral in seconds!" Jagger Stephen ordered, stepping closer to get a better angle for his phone's video recorder.

"A deal is a deal, right, Aiden?" asked his Hockey Day coach.

Aiden pointed his finger at his coach and stated, "Can I tug on it?"

"Bhaaaaaaa," the coach replied, jostling Aiden. The entire hotel lobby erupted in laughter.

"Wildest beard on Hockey Day! That's one amazing coach," said Ref Rosee.

As hockey continued, friendships were the top-shelf breakaway on this Hockey Day.

CHAPTER 7

Hockey Day, The Holiday

Months had passed since Hockey Day and the piles of snow were beginning to melt. Hockeytown, USA had wrapped up their winning season. Moms and dads were beginning to make their kids' annual summer plans.

Cullen, Luke, Jagger Stephen, and McLaren were heading back for another month-long adventure at Minnesota

Hockey Camps. Avery and Paisley were excited to join Coach Lamoureux in Detroit Lakes for a girls' hockey school of champions, teaming up to teach Learn to Skate lessons all summer.

Ann and Blaine had decided to stay close to home with weekly summer practices for the Minnesota Bears. The dazzling duo, along with Aiden, were going to be busy all summer, modeling for an upcoming hockey equipment ad.

Biggest of all in everyone's minds, however, was a different kind of hockey celebration.

"Culleeennn! Cuulllllleenn!" Blaine yelled loudly.

Cullen woke suddenly, rolled over in his hotel bed, and looked at his brother.

"What?" he asked, stretching himself upright.

Blaine was standing in front of the room's mirror, looking at the neon-orange bow tie twisted around his neck.

"Here, lil bro," Cullen said, reaching over and correctly fastening the bow tie.

"Illlllll loooookkkk handsome," Blaine proudly proclaimed.

"Minus a few wrinkles in your shirt," Cullen punched back, straightening the shirt and holding his brother's shoulder.

"Bigggggg ddayy," Blaine said.

"Every day is a big day with you. You get excited about the silliest stuff. I love you, Blaine," Cullen said, ruffling his brother's hair.

"Boys, you ready to go? Your teammates are sitting in the lobby waiting!" their dad called from the adjourning room.

"Holy breezers and frozen hockey pucks," Avery mumbled while taking pictures of the Governor's office.

"I think 'Senator Lukey' has a nice ring to it," Luke told his team as they took a seat on the Governor's couch.

"Not as nice of a ring as 'Governor Paisley,'" Avery shot back, high-fiving Paisley.

"I'll be too busy playing for Team USA in the Olympics to run a political campaign," Cullen countered. The team giggled, a sound that abruptly faded away when a young man in a suit strode into the room.

"The Governor is ready for the proclamation signing; please follow me," stated the young assistant.

The team and their parents slowly

walked into the Governor's press room. Paisley took a deep breath. Avery's mouth dropped at the sight of the antique chandelier. Blaine grabbed his mom's hand after seeing the line-up of television cameras ready to film the announcement.

The Governor, after the usual waving and shaking of hands, moved to the microphone.

"Every day is a great day for hockey. I thank these young players for writing to me and asking for Hockey Day to be recognized as an official Minnesota holiday. Minnesota is the State of Hockey; hockey is for everyone, and today we are making it official," stated the Governor as he signed the proclamation.

The press began to ask questions.

"Cullen? What does Hockey Day mean to you?" a reporter asked.

Cullen smiled and looked at his brother. "Seeing my little brother play hockey and knowing hockey is for everyone."

"Ann? What does Hockey Day mean to you?" asked another reporter.

Ann looked at her mom. "Go ahead, Ann," her mom encouraged.

"I love hockey. I love my friends more. I want to be my team's captain next year and when I grow up I want to be the announcer for Hockey Day!" Ann said, beaming.

"Hired!" the Governor interjected.

"To me, hockey is awesome and means friendship," Aiden typed on his home computer to Jagger Stephen and McLaren.

"Right back at ya, buddy," Jagger Stephen typed.

Jagger Stephen and McLaren clicked

off their internet connection. "Super cool
to watch the proclamation signing live
with Chop Chop via computer. Hockey
friendships rock!"

Hooray for Hockey Day!

STATE *of* MINNESOTA

WHEREAS:	The popularity of hockey in Minnesota is well established.
WHEREAS:	Most kids in Minnesota are introduced to skating and hockey at an early age; on the frozen ponds, lakes and rivers.
WHEREAS:	In Minnesota, the State of Hockey is a symbol of heritage and Minnesota has produced more professional players than any other state.
WHEREAS:	In Minnesota the blood's in your game, and we truly eat sleep and breathe hockey.
WHEREAS:	Minnesota is the State of Hockey.

NOW, THEREFORE, I, MARK DAYTON, Governor of Minnesota and former college goalie, do hereby proclaim April 1 as:

"HOCKEY DAY" AN OFFICIAL HOLIDAY

in the State of Minnesota.

IN WITNESS WHEREOF, I have hereunto set my hand and caused the Great Seal of the State of Minnesota to be affixed at the State Capitol this 2nd day of February.

_____
GOVERNOR

_____
SECRETARY OF STATE

ASK THE OFFICIALS
Rylee and Rosee's
Referee Resources

Important Words to Learn

Antarctica: earth's southernmost continent and site of the South Pole

cherry picking: loafing or floating in ice hockey; the floater (a player) literally casually skates behind the opposing team's defenseman

etiquette: code of polite behavior

Governor: the elected executive or head of state

guffaw: a loud and boisterous laugh

ice sledge hockey: a special kind of hockey that allows players with disabilities to compete; players use metal frames to move across the ice

Jeremy Roenick: An American former professional ice hockey player who played the majority of his career in the National Hockey League (NHL). He played for the Chicago Blackhawks, Phoenix Coyotes, Philadelphia Flyers, Los Angeles Kings, and San Jose Sharks over the course of his eighteen-season NHL career, and represented Team USA in numerous international tournaments.

persistence: firm continuance in a course of action

petition: a formal written request

proclamation: the Governor will issue proclamations for extraordinary state or local events that deserve special recognition

rut: a deep crack in the ice

sudden death: traditionally has been used in hockey playoff and championship games

trepidation: wariness, reluctance

Warroad Gardens: 70,000-ft. square arena featuring an Olympic-size ice sheet, eight locker rooms, and over 1,454 theater-style seats, located in Warroad, MN (Hockeytown, USA)

MEET JAYNE AND KATRINA

Jayne wears many helmets, including college professor, lawyer, author, and entrepreneur of fun. "Team Beehler" enjoys a hockey game every night.

Katrina shares her high energy and love for all things creative as an artist, designer, decorator, illustrator, art educator, event planner, wife, mother, and hardware store owner.

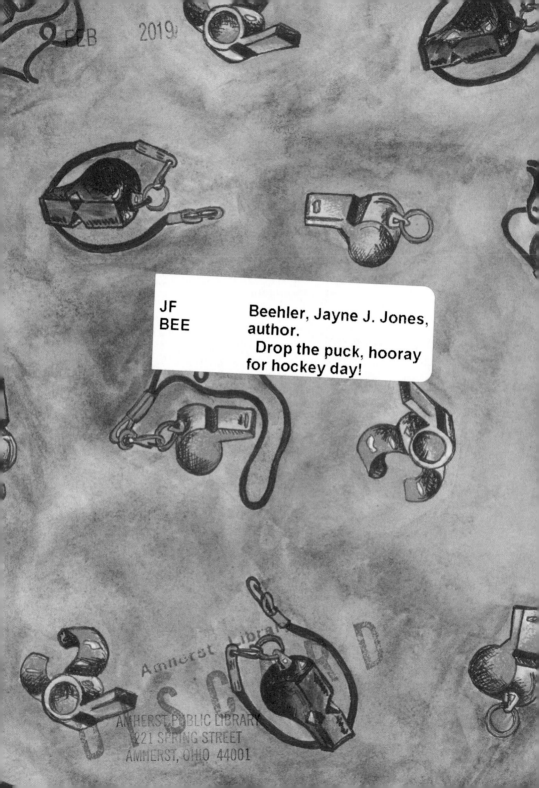